Jay G:
Assignment to
The Netherlands

John Gumbs

Published by John Gumbs
Publishing partner: Paragon Publishing, Rothersthorpe
First published 2020
© John Gumbs 2020, London

ISBN 978-1-78222-782-3

Book design, layout and production management by Into Print
www.intoprint.net
+44 (0)1604 832149

Contents

1

The Case in Nijmegen

JAY G WAS called into the Detective office in Nottingham, and told that he had a new assignment. He was given a brown packet which he opened and began to read. He pushed his face up when he saw the place where he was going to. Three days he was given to prepare himself, to get his transport and to be away.

Jay G wondered now if his wife and son would like the idea. They would have to swot up some to learn a bit of the language where they were going. He left the detective office and went to the town. Catching a bus that would take him home, he sat down still thinking hard about the assignment. Jay G looked at the country's name, and it was the Netherlands, the place he had to get himself to was called Nijmegen. There he would work with the Dutch Police on the case that had been going on for three years. Coming off the bus, he made his way down the street in front of him, walked to the first street to his left, and then took that one. A few meters on his left was his residence. His wife was just about to go shopping, his son was at school which wasn't that far away, just around the corner.

Jay G stepped into the house and started telling his wife about their leaving Nottingham and going to the Netherlands.

"Do we have to dress up and wear clogs as well?" she asked.

Jay G took her, and they sat down in the living room.

"No, it's not like that. We as foreigners can wear what we like. Not everyone walks about in clogs. Don't worry about that! We are only going there for three months."

"What about the language?" she wanted to know.

"Don't worry about that," Jay G told her. "Most of the European countries speak English."

Jay G left his wife after giving her information about their trip overseas. He often, when he is home, and it was the end of the school day, go and accompany his son home.

Going down the street to the corner shop he was suddenly stopped in his tracks when two youths sped out the shop, going left down the other road. Jay G ran behind them grabbing his mobile and sending a message back to the office. Down a lane they went, and into an old abandoned building two storeys high, with rusty railings lying at the side. The building must have been some sort of factory or warehouse.

Jay G eased his way in, listening for sounds. On his left, cemented steps led to the floor above. He came to the top, and reaching a broken door, he tried to open it. Then as he entered, an iron bar came down upon him that had let loose from the side of the wall. He managed somehow to avoid the full force of the bar, but was still a little hurt. A van from the office was already outside the building.

Inside the building the two youths aged about 17 years came at Jay G trying to overpower him. Jay G realized that he had to defend himself, or he would end up being more badly hurt. He grabbed one of the youths, pulled him hard into him, moved away, and the youth went straight into the wall, and sliding down to the floor hurt. The next kid ran away downstairs and was picked up by those waiting outside.

There was blood coming from where the iron bar had fallen on Jay G; it wasn't that bad, and a bandage was placed on the wound.

*

Back at his home, Jay G's son had already arrived back from school. His wife, when she saw Jay G, said, "You're hurt!"

"It's nothing much," he said, and turned to his son. "How was it in school today?" His son said that everything went well.

At the Nottingham Midland Airport Jay G was there with his family waiting for the flight to the Netherlands. Not far away from where they were, was the WC, and he went there, leaving his wife and son seated in the waiting place.

Jay G was alone in the WC up at the left where the urine bowls were. With his back turned to the entrance, he hadn't seen when the big man came through the door. He turned around to his left but it was too late. The right fist of the big man came crashing through the right side of Jay G. He sunk low, moving quickly to the left, with speed, he went into the big man shoving him back into the middle area. The main door opened, and that's when the big man hurried away out of it. Jay G felt the pain in his right side, but he could still move himself.

Outside in the waiting area, his wife and son looked at him as if they were seeing a stranger. He sat down beside them for a few minutes more without telling them what had taken place in the WC. The call came for passengers to board their plane to the Netherlands. Jay G, along with his wife and son went out through the gate and boarded the plane.

The flight wasn't long, just over one hour and twenty minutes. The plane came down and landed. Transport was already waiting to take Jay G and his family away. The story had already gone out that a detective was coming from England to help in the case. The journey from the airport to Nijmegen was pleasant, and they arrived and got into their apartment opposite Kronenburg park, and not so very far from the Police

Station. Jay G's wife and son liked the place so that was okay.

The following day, Jay G went for briefing. He was taken up to the place where they found the body, not very far from the Nijmegen bridge. Jay G looked around, examining the area well. He noticed the barges going up and down carrying their load up to Germany.

The Dutch detective turned to Jay G and said, "We almost had this case wrapped up, but the killer slipped away."

Jay G said, "We'll soon take care of that. Any idea where we could start?" They both left the area under the bridge, and went along it looking at the scenery. "I must say," Jay G started, "nice scenery you have here!"

"Quite amazing, isn't it?" Detective Loemann said.

Jay G was shown the waterfront, up and beyond the bridge with the row of houses on the opposite side. Not far from the bridge were many houseboats. Below them was a big steamer waiting for passengers. At the borttom was the main rail bridge with the bicycle path beside it. Detective Loemann told Jay G that the people were very friendly and peaceful; and that he must not deal too hard, a heavy hand.

Jay G gave a big grin. "I know what you mean!"

Detective Loemann went on to say, "We've never had any real trouble here."

After this, Jay G went back to his place.

That same night Jay G went out snooping. He was down at the house boats just below the bridge. Going up on the boardwalk, he came to a boat with its door ajar. No one was around so he went down and into the boat.

Looking around he found a drawer with an album. He shuffled quickly through the pages until one photo caught his eye. It was the photo of the British man and a young girl at the circus. As soon as he took hold of the photo to take it out the album, he heard a sound, and quickly laid low.

Holding the small torch tightly in his hand, he waited.

Then he heard the voice of a middle-aged woman say,

"I know that you are in there, who are you? What do you want?"

The lighting came on. Jay G couldn't do anything because there were not any places to hide. The woman made her way in and said, "Get out, or I call the police."

"I am a police detective," Jay G told her. "Maybe you could help me. It has to do with the British man who was murdered three years ago."

She blurted out, *"I had nothing to do with it.* I only met him that one time at the circus."

"Tell me some more what happened at the circus."

"I have already given statement of what happened," she said.. "I'm clear of having anything to do with it."

"If you don't mind, I'd like to hear it from you."

She sat down on one of the small canvas chairs and said, "It was about two in the afternoon when I bumped into him. He was a nice chap, spoke fluent Dutch, and invited me for a ride in the circular tubes. I accepted."

"And then what?"

"Later in the afternoon – much later – we came back here, had a few drinks, and then he left."

"Did you see where he went?"

"I didn't leave the boat."

Jay G said, "Thanks for your help," and turned to leave, when she said, "I remembered him telling me about some friends he had on Hertogstraat, a bar not far from here."

"How do I get there?"

"Just walk about 50 meters, then take the steps to your left, there are many. At the top walk directly to the street in front of you. That's it!" she told him.

As Jay G turned again to leave, he came face to face with Karl, the boyfriend of the woman. Karl was a rough, tough man, and he wasn't in the mood right now to make friends with Jay G.

He jammed Jay G in the small doorway. The woman shouted out, *"KARL!"* But it was too late. Karl sunk to the floor from a barrage of left and rights he received from Jay G.

Jay G stepped onto the boardwalk, and went away.

Following the directions he was given, he came to the street with its many bars. The third bar along on the left was the one he wanted. It was *The Cozy Bar*. He stepped inside, and ordered a drink, a soft one. There were a few people in, and the juke box was busy playing. The old barman eyed up Jay G, for he had never seen him before.

"Are you new in this town?" the barman asked.

"I arrived here not long ago. Nice town you have here," Jay G said.

"It is the oldest in Netherlands from Roman times."

"Oh! I see," Jay G took the photo he had, showed it to the barman. "Seen this man before?"

"That's the man who got killed years ago. Do you know him? He was a regular customer."

"Carry on," Jay G said, "sounds interesting!"

"Well, he had a girlfriend, they both came here often. Then I heard that they split up, and there was some trouble over that, then they found hm down by the bridge. Awful!"

"His girlfriend, does she still come here?"

"I haven't seen her for a long time."

Jay G knocked back the rest of his drink, said thanks to the barman and left.

He walked along some more on the street, turned right and went down past the bank, down to the restaurant on the corner, turned right, walked down to the square, then straight down to Kroneburg park. As he was crossing the park, he came close to a bench, it was now getting dark, and one of the homeless there on the bench, roused himself when he saw he had company. Jay G was alert, ready to defend himself from any attack. The homeless man just fell back on the bench when he realized that Jay G was no use to him.

Jay G got home and his wife and son were glad to see him arrive in one piece.

The next evening around 8 pm, Jay G went down to the bar that was located not so far away from him, and just across from the Kronenburg park. Inside the bar there were a few people, some playing a game of dice, and others just hanging about. The bar wasn't like one of those back home, Jay G noticed. It was sort of *too* peaceful, with everyone enjoying themselves. The big bar man eyed Jay G up and asked if he wanted a drink. Jay G ordered a soft drink, went and sat down in a chair just behind a young woman of 20.

The young woman turned and said to Jay G, "I've never seen you in here before!"

"That's right! I'm new. Just passing a few minutes away. And you, are you a regular?"

"Always here on the Wednesday, and the weekends."

Jay G took out the photo and showed it to her.

"Have you ever seen him before?"

Her face lit up. "Well, yes, I spoke with him many times at the weekends. He came in with a girl. I've heard about what happened."

"It was unfortunate for him," Jay G told her. "Seems like he ran into trouble."

"Are you some kind of detective?" she asked, giving back the photo.

"I am from England, came over to help on this case. Did you know anything else about him?"

"Not really! He seemed to be a nice person."

"Okay, thanks," Jay G said, and got up to leave.

"Leaving so early?" she asked. "I was just getting used to you."

"Have work to do ... and I am married!"

Jay G left the place, not seeing the two men who followed after him. As he got to the bus stop, just opposite the park, they tackled him, and got him quickly across the road and into the park beneath the dark shade of the trees lining the road.

Jay G manage to say, "Who are you? What do you want?"

He's playing it cool, hoping he would not have to fight his way out. The two chaps were of medium build, just about the same size as Jay G himself. They said to him, "Karl is our brother, and you're going to be paid back for what you have done to him."

"He was the one who attacked me first, I had to defend myself."

They took Jay G across the small dirt track that went through the park, and down to the duck pond. They struggled, but they managed to get his head under water. Jay G was lucky because at that time, an old couple were walking their dog out. The two men, when they saw the couple, let go of Jay G, and went away.

Jay G caught his breath, shook his head a few times left to right. Soaking wet, he went out the park, and to his apartment.

2

Jay G Snooping Around

JAY G NOW had to do some of his own work that he was accustomed to, in order to get information.

The next day at the Police station, Jay G told all that had taken place. They told him to take it easy no matter what happened. But Jay G wasn't one of those who can go easy, especially when he's on a case. Arms, ribs and other body parts will get broken during his investigations. How can one take it easy? In every country there are criminals, and Jay G never takes it easy with them.

Just before evening time when the traffic was light, and after looking out at the place of the incident, from the bridge, Jay G walked along slowly. Three men came along on bikes and surrounded him. At the same time there was a police car with two policemen. They slowed down when they saw the men. Coming over to where Jay G was, the men rode away on their bikes. Jay G got a ride back across the bridge.

He realized now while working on the case that he had many enemies. Now he knows he has to watch out for himself, be alert. That evening, he went up by the old church where there was a bar down in a cellar. It was always jam packed. You had to go down a few steps, and then there was the circular bar.

Jay G squeezed his way around until he found a space right at the back, and was able to speak to one of those helping in the bar. Jay G had no plans in staying in this bar for long. He took the photo he had, and showed it to one of the helpers at the the bar. He remembered seeing the face, but didn't know him personally.

Jay G managed to make his way out of the bar, after thanking the helper. Halfway round, trying to make a way through, Jay G saw over the other side a man also making his way hurriedly to get to the steps. They both got to the first step at the same time. Jay G didn't hesitate, he grabbed the man, and half lifted him up the steps until they were both out the door.

Taking him aside where an arch way was, leading into the grounds of the church, Jay G questioned him. "Who are you? And why were you looking at me the way you did? Do you know who I am? And why I am here?"

The man, still half out of breath and smelling of beer, said, "I know who you are, and why you are here. You're on that case of that British man. I saw him walking along one day along the waal, and he went into a house not far from the railbridge."

"Did you see the number of the house?"

"I think it was 25 or 23."

"Thanks for the information. And if you think of anything else, I'll always be around here from time to time," Jay G told the man, and walked away from him.

The next day, Jay G went down the waal and started snooping around. He came to the houses numbered 25 and 23. He wasn't absolutely sure which one it was. Pushing the door bell of 25, he waited a few minutes, then he saw a man coming out from another door and running away. Jay G went after him, half stumbling over the cobbled mounds that were placed there. Chasing the man down the waal, until they came to where the road turned left, and there before him were steps leading up to the bicycle track with the train track next to it on the left. Jay G was not far behind his man. They got to the top and Jay G was surprised when the man went over into the track of the train. A few minutes later a train came by, and Jay G had no idea where the man went. He was sure that he wasn't run over by the train. Jay G sat down on the top of the steps, and was angry with himself for not running faster and overtaking his man. But that's the way it sometime happens in this game. Feeling a bit better after that chase, he slowly went back down the steps, went back to the house, but found nothing.

Two days later, Jay G is walking down to a famous bar He stepped inside and saw the beautiful woman there. She was the owner of the place. Jay G had seen many beautiful women while he was a detective, but that's all – he was a married man and had no intention of messing around. She gave him a pretty smile as he got to the bar and ordered what he wanted. There were only a few people in. Staying at the bar, Jay G began talking with the woman, taking out the photo and showing it to her. She took the photo and immediately recognized the face. "That's that British man," she said. "He came in here quite often."

"Was he alone?"

"He used to come in with a girl, they did that regularly," she told Jay G.

"Describe the girl to me!"

The description that the woman gave stayed as a clear picture to Jay G.

"I think they must have broken up because he came in many weeks alone," the woman said.

"Was he a friendly chap?"

"He seemed okay to me, always smiling and joking. There are many more people who knew him personally. You can find them in here on the weekends!"

"Thanks!" Jay G said, and left. Outside he saw the sign board *Annette's Bar.* He had now visited a number of bars, knew where they all were, and could get himself around without getting lost. It was enough for the day, so he went back to his own place, to his wife and son.

The following week on a weekend, Jay G talked with a number of people who knew George, the British man. He learned about the girlfriend he had and later split up The address was given to him of the young woman, and decided to pay her a visit. She wasn't living far from the waal. Jay G had already visited the one on the boat house, and heard what she had to say.

Outside the door, Jay G pushed the bell and waited. A pretty young woman opened the door and said, "Yes?"

Jay G took his identification badge, and showed it. "I'm detective Jay G. Is it possible to ask you a few questions?"

"About what?" she asked. Jay G took the photo, holding it, he showed it to her. As soon as she saw the photo, she began to close the door. Jay G pleaded with her to stay. She listened to Jay G, but she told him she wanted no more to do with this. It is all behind her.

Jay G said, "I know how you feel, I would have reacted the same way too. I'm sorry to bring this up, but it is rather important to hear from you certain things. I read what you said to the police, but maybe, I was thinking, you'd forgotten something."

She opened the door wider, and invited Jay G in. "Would you like some coffee or something to drink?" she asked him.

"No thanks," he said, and started questioning her. Marlene sat there with a cup of coffee. Jay G said, "Tell me about George!"

"There's nothing much to tell really, only that we were in a relationship for a short while, then I broke it off."

"Why did you do that? Was there something wrong? I read in your report that he started smoking. What do you mean by that?"

"You know ... *smoking*," she said, "to get yourself high."

"I get what you mean. You didn't tell this in your report, you only said smoking."

"That is the term we use mostly when referring to that stuff."

"Where would he get that stuff from?" Jay G asked her.

"You know, from those people who deal in it."

Jay G knew now that George had got himself in deep trouble with this business. It was dangerous, even dangerous to talk about it. It was not easy to get to the leader or who it was that was running the whole operation. Well organized, they delivered their stuff to their customers without any hint of where it came from. "Do you think," Jay G asked her, "that George was involved in some way?"

"That's one of the reasons why we broke up, I would have none of it."

"What about names, did he mention any?"

"He did mention a Victor who came now and then to Annette's bar."

Jay G thanked Marlene for her help and time, then left.

Annette's bar had many people in it when Jay G turned up. He walked in, got a quick drink, and walked back out again. It was strange why he acted that way. Outside to his left, a sports car pulled up, and someone from inside the bar went to the car. Jay G heard the name Victor and immediately moved down to the car. He saw that the driver had given the person who came to him, a small packet.

As the driver was getting beack into his car, Jay G said, "Victor, could you get me some stuff?"

"Who are you?" Victor inquired. "Never seen you around here before!"

"Oh! I'm new, just moved into the area, not far from here."

"How did you know my name?" he wanted to know.

"Some of your mates told me about you when they heard I wanted some stuff."

"It's not cheap," he told Jay G. "Yes, I can get you some. You have to keep it quiet."

"I'm good at keeping secrets, you can trust me."

Jay G behaved himself in a way that he didn't cause Victor to suspect anything. And the clothes Jay G was wearing were nothing fancy. Many people were wearing the same. Jay G had a good look at Victor. He was turning around 25, had a well-built figure, with two scars on his face.

The street they were on was leading down to the waal, and only the light from over the bar shown directly on the sidewalk below. Victor's car was just below the bar in the dark. As Victor turned to get into the car, Jay G grabbed him, and flung him heavily against the building. There was no one around at that time. Victor cried out, *"MAN, WHAT'RE YOU DOING?"* Jay G had him in a hold in which he couldn't get away.

"I want some answers from you, and pretty quick. Do you know George, the British man, you gave him stuff often? Who is your supplier?"

Jay G was digging in knowing that he wouldn't get a direct answer.

"George?" Victor repeated. "Who is George? I don't know who you're talking about."

"The British guy who got killed not far from the bridge."

"I had nothing to do with that ... I ..."

Jay G tightened the grip.

"You *DO* know something about it."

Suddenly someone came out the bar, saw to his left what was going on, came down only to face Jay G, who moved so fast, shoving Victor to the ground, and grabbed the other. Victor was trying to tackle Jay G's feet, but Jay G shuffled away, and flung the other man also to the ground. Jay G grabbed Victor again, took him away from the bar, down into the dark of the street, got him against a wooden building, and started questioning him again. Victor finally told him who had given him the order. Jay G learned quite a lot more of what was going on. He had to get the police in, for it was now getting very dangerous. He had already made contact with the police just before he came into contact with Victor. It wasn't long before a police car and a van was there. Jay G explained to them what had been going on. Victor was taken in for questioning.

An address had already been given to Jay G.

3

Jay G in Dead Trouble

THE ADDRESS JAY G had that Victor had given him was a few kilometers away. He was told that the man was very dangerous. Jay G as a detective never carried a gun. Jay G was always in contact with the police office just in case he needed more help. He decided to see first how it went down, and if it got out of hand, he would get backup. The few kilometers, he decided would do him good. Under the rail bridge he went, having the old paper building on his right. The path led along some docks, then over and down to some buildings on his left. Curtains were half drawn on the window next to the door. Jay G went up and pushed the bell. He waited. Nothing, he pushed it again, and this time it opened. This man appeared like one of those Samurai wrestlers. Jay G already had his badge and the photo to show the man. The man didn't want to stay any longer at the door and started closing it. Jay G put a foot to stop him from doing so. The man became angry, opened the door again, and grabbbed a hold onto Jay G, at the same time, the police cars were there. It's hard to say if Jay G was lucky or not. What would have happened if the police cars weren't there? Jay G was no fool, he could handle himself, and although this bloke had a few pounds, he didn't scare Jay G off.

Jay G was down at the spot just a few meters from the bridge, where they had found the British man. There was a sandy spot, then grass all around, and down to the water's edge, many stones. He had been to this place many times, and for some unknown reason, there was something bothering him. At that particular moment, he just couldn't figure it out. Jay G knew as well, he should not be working alone, because things had now become more dangerous. Coming down from the steps of the bridge, Jay G saw the three men, they were coming directly towards him. He had his back towards the water, and had already planned what he was going to do. The smallest one was a bit to his right, while the other two were in front of him. Jay G moved fast, knocking down the chap that was to his right, and headed for the steps of the bridge.

With all his strength he flew up those steps, then along the bicycle pedestrian track, until he got to the middle of the bridge. In front of him was the main traffic. The men coming from his right was also in full force. Jay went upon the beam that was running along level with the bicycle track, only a bit higher. Luck was in for Jay G because as he stood upright on the beam, below in the water, a long barge with a heavy load of sand came under the bridge going up river. Jay G flung himself over, and landed on the sand, it hurt him, but didn't do much damage. He looked back when the barge had left the bridge, only to see his enemies looking amazed.

Further up the river, the barge came in close to the edge, then turned for the middle of the water. Jay G knew he had the chance now to get off. He did so, but ended up soaking wet. Moving through the thick grass and small trees, he made his way out to the road leading to Germany, and back to the place where he should be. The big round-a-bout was about 2 kilometers away.

*

The wife of Jay G opened the door and stared at the mess he was in. At the briefing the following day, Jay G was given two policemen who would be in their car, and close to where he was. Should things get too hot, they could call for more help, and assist in anyway they could.

Later in that day Jay G was on Hertogstraat. The bar that was on the corner adjoining Grote Walstraat was always packed, no matter what day it was. Jay G walked in, and saw immediately how the woman behind the bar smiled at him.

"Already taken," he told her, and took out the photo. She took it from him, looking at it, she said, "I know him. Unfortunate of what took place. He came in here often, everyone liked him."

"Was he alone?"

"He was with a girl!"

Jay took the photo, looked around a bit, and was just about to leave when this guy came up to him.

"You look like one of those private police people!"

"You mean a private detective. Have you got news for me?"

"I happen to see the photo. I know the guy."

"Come on, tell me more!"

"Not in here," the man told Jay G, "let's go outside."

Outside the bar, on the Grote Waal straat, the man started telling Jay G what he knew. Not far away, in the police car, were two policemen. They found it strange the way Jay G worked. But he was getting the information he needed, and was sifting out his enemies. They knew that they were there in case things got hot. A couple more chaps followed out from the bar, and as soon the man with Jay G saw them, he ran away up the road.

Jay G went after him, and the other two men also. The police car took the other street leading up to the roundabout and the park. Reaching the green kiosk, the man who was talking with Jay G, looked back, and at the same time was grabbed by Jay G, and took into the dark behind a tree.

The other two men came past the kiosk, and as they came near to the tree where Jay G and the man were, Jay G came out furiously into the two men knocking them over on the ground.

The two policemen were there on the spot, but they didn't arrest the two men. There were no charges against them. Jay G took the other man and left the park.

Jay G got lots of information from the man who was with him. He said that he knew the British man, had a drink many times with him; that he was a nice fellow; and had seen him with one or two girlfriends. Jay G was given an address not far from the Railway Station where the British man had lodged.

Outside, the three-story building, Jay G was looking for an entrance. After a while, he found it, and slid in through the small door. Steps were leading upwards, and Jay G took them, reaching to the floor where there was an office. The woman behind the big desk looked up and said to Jay G, "Can I help you?"

"I'm a private detective, and I heard that this person was living here at one time." Jay G took the photo and showed it. The woman pulled out a drawer on the right of her, looked through, and came out with a folder. She opened it and spread it on the desk. She told Jay G exactly when the British man had come there and when he left. More, she didn't know. Jay G thanked the woman and left. He was thinking back now of the information the man had given him. First, he'll go to the police briefing, then start making some serious plans. The man had told him about a man who came well-dressed in a fancy car, and he was pretty sure the man was a criminal. Jay G knew where he had to go, and he wasted no time.

*

Just outside the big main bank, he crossed the road, turned to his left, and along until he came to a blue house. There was a drive in the front with a car parked to the right. Two steps led up to a wooden frame veranda. The police car wasn't far away. Jay G went up to the front door, pushed the bell and waited. It wasn't long before the door opened, and a slim man appeared. Jay G already had the badge and the photo in his hand showing it to the man. The man looked at the photo then shook his head, "Never seen him before!"

"But you took his money. You're lying. He came to this very house to do business with you."

"I'm afraid you have to leave now," the man told Jay G.

"Not until you tell me what's been going on. Who are you working for?"

Jay G pushed the man aside, and stepped inside only to find that the man wasn't alone. The man quickly closed the door, and Jay G found himself with three other men there. Jay G knew that the police car was outside, not far away, keeping a watch on him. He had his mobile with him, and it was one of those where you only have to press a button. And this can be done while still in the pocket. The men were terribly angry with Jay G, didn't like the way he barged in on them. They came closer to him. Looking at him from head to foot, then sniggered at him. One of them said, "Can't you see that you're easy meat for us? You're crazy trying to take us all by yourself."

"Is that so," Jay G said, and lashed out with such speed and power that two of them were already down on their knees. He pushed the slim man aside, went to the door, and gave a signal to the police car. They came, entered the building, looking around to see if the law had been broken. There was nothing that they could find so they left giving Jay G a lift.

4

Two Days in Amsterdam

A WEEK LATER, Jay G was on a train headed for Amsterdam. It would take about one hour. Standing outside the Amsterdam Railway Station, Jay G turned right with the tourist boats on his right, and in front of him all the tram lines. He waited for a tram to pass, and then he crossed the street. The big hotel was there in front of him. Jay G went in and booked a room. He went back out, walked a few meters more and came to a narrow street which took him up to a small bridge crossing the water. Jay G noticed that there were quite many of these bridges in Amsterdam. On top of this one as he crossed over were many bicycles here and there on both sides of the bridge. Getting to the end of the bridge on his right, was a four-storey building, the bottom part was a bar; but it was also a place where you can smoke and get stuff. Jay G stepped into the place, and found that he could hardly seem to breathe from the smoke that was floating around. He was held immediately by two well-built men who forced him back outside, and had him against the railing that was there as safety to prevent falling into the water.

"Who are you?" they asked him.

"Do you *really* want to know?" he asked them. With great speed, Jay G jerked his arms away from both men, at the same time giving them a push so that they fell through the gap between the railings, and over into the water. Jay G went back over the bridge, and was gone.

*

The two policemen who were given to him in Nijmegen could not accompany him to Amsterdam, but Jay G had contact with the police there, and knew what to do if he needed help. Jay G was a very good detective, his eyes never let him down, and he always had this right feeling of what to do and when to do it. Jay G had taken things seriously at the Police Academy when he was in training, he knew that at times he would get into serious trouble, and that it was important to get himself out of it. He learned how to defend himself, attack and retreat, without hurting himself. A man had been following him when he first arrived and went to book his hotel. Jay G had no intention of staying at that hotel. Another place was found.

There was a stand with hot dogs, and he grabbed himself a quick bite. After doing so, he prepared himself to go to the next address. Jay G knew his way around, and was keeping track of where he had been, and where he had to go to. He had been briefed back in Nijmegen about the 'coffee shops' – it didn't appeal to him, but that was the custom. As he came to the end of the road he was on, he saw the sign "coffee". He went in and sat down hoping to get a nice cup of coffee. The bloke came over and said to Jay G, *"What kind of stuff do you want?"*

Jay G looked at him, and said, "You're under arrest for trafficking illegal stuff."

The bloke said, "Man, you're in the wrong place, get the hell out. This coffee shop is legal."

Jay G got up and went outside, knowing he had been in the wrong place to get coffee. He finally found a restaurant, and was able to get what he wanted.

Being now refreshed, Jay G took a side street, walked along it for sometime, turned right, and came to the address he wanted.

*

Jay G waited for a few minutes before he pushed the bell. A servant lady opened the door.

"I'm looking for Mt. Rolemann," Jay G said.

"One moment!" she told him, and went away. A few seconds later, a man came to the door. He looked like a business man with a cigar in his right hand. Just a bit shorter than Jay G.

"Can I help you?" he said.

"Could you spare me a few minutes, I'm a private detective."

"Come on in. What is this all about?" He took Jay G across the room, and into a big posh office. He showed Jay G a chair, while he sat in the one opposite.

Jay G took out the photo, and placed it on the desk in front of Mr. Rolemann.

"I'm investigating the case of the British man who got killed in Nijmegen, by the main bridge. He got caught up in the drugs racket."

"Am I supposed to know this man? What has he got to do with me?"

"Some of your servants, I'm afraid, have squealed on you. I'm not here to waste my time nor yours. Is there anything you can tell me?"

"I think that you are wasting your time talking to me, for I know absolutely nothing. Don't know what you're talking about."

"Were you ever living in Nijmegen?"

"Yes, I lived there ten years, nice people. Then I came here to Amsterdam."

Jay G leaned forward, "Well, let me remind you that when you were back there in Nijmegen, you were involved in a shady business. And that's where the British man comes in. Did you have anything to do with it?"

"Don't be preposterous to think that I would drop so low!"

"So you're not accepting having anything to do with it?" Jay G asked him.

"Absolutely!"

"I will tell you that you had men working for you, and I've got some information that you were in the business. Young people have died because of you, and you're telling me, you had nothing to do with it!"

The man got up from his chair. At the same time a door behind Jay G opened. He turned around to see a big Asian man standing there. Mr. Rolemann gave the Asian a sign, and he came towards Jay G. Being careful, Jay G got from his chair quickly. He had been taught how to deal with people who have a few more pounds than himself in body weight. Jay G grabbed the chair he had been sitting in, and brought it over his head smashing it into the Asian man. That didn't hurt him. Trying to get a hold on Jay G, he moved heavily. Jay G was tall, well-built, and could move very quickly which he did, not letting the Asian man get a hold on him. That was his main aim, to get a hold on Jay G. But Jay G had other plans. Jay G got some space between the Asian man and himself, and rushed into him sideways, knocking him awkwardly over and onto the floor.

Mr. Rolemann came from behind his desk and tried to attack Jay G only to find himself too, on the ground with the quick movement Jay G made. Jay G held him fast, watching carefully the movement of the Asian, as he tried to raise himself from the ground in pain. Jay G took Mr. Rolemann around to the desk. "I need a name, come on, let's have it!"

Mr. Rolemann managed to say, "Gerard ... Dellen ... That's all I know."

Jay G let him go, walked away, looked at the Asian, still there in pain, opened the door, and found his way outside.

5

Confrontation near the Border

BACK IN NIJMEGEN Jay G opened the telephone book, and started looking for the name he was given by Mr. Rolemann. He found there were a few pages with the name Dellen, but finally he came to the one he wanted. He noted the number and the address. Using his mobile to show him where the address was, he followed the directions carefully. He walked along the waal, and stood outside the boathouse of the woman who had been friends with the British man. Planning to pay her a visit, he changed his mind. Instead, he walked a few kilometers, and came to the main bus station. He took the right bus and got himself where he wanted to. Once he was off the bus, he walked a few meters, and then turned left. The two policemen in their police car could have taken Jay G where he wanted to go, but he preferred doing it his way. They were there anyway, in case he needed help.

After turning left, Jay G walked down to a house that was at the bottom, and close to the edge of the wood. Over the bell button was the name *Gerard Dellen*. The space in front the house was rather large. Jay G moved up to push the bell, and in doing so, a man came from the right side of the house, looked at Jay G and said, "Are you looking for me?"

Jay G said, "If you're Mr. Gerard Dellen, yes. I'm a private detective." Jay G took out the badge and photo, gave it to Dellen. He looked at it, shook his head.

"No, doesn't ring a bell to me."

What Jay G didn't know was that Mr. Rolemann had already phoned Dellen, and told him what had happened in Amsterdam, and that he Rolemann was forced to give Dellen's address. Jay G wasn't stupid, neither was Dellen. He had already made plans how he was going to handle Jay G. The two policemen were out of his sight, and he thought that Jay G had turned up alone.

"You must have read about what happened?" Jay G said.

"That is possible," Dellen said, "but there's no connection between myself and that man."

"I think there is, and I'm going to prove it," Jay G told Dellen.

"You're not going to prove anything," Dellen said, and pulled out his gun, pointing it to Jay G.

It was now becoming dark, and Jay G was led down a small track, and deeper into the woods. This was a moment where Jay G had to be very careful. He had to follow his enemy's orders, especially when a gun was pointed at him. The two policemen got a signal from Jay G's mobile, left their car, and came down the track leading to the woods. It was now dark, and they called up for more help.

Dellen took Jay G deeper in the woods, keeping Jay G well covered. They came to a small gutter, and Jay G was planning to make his move. He couldn't dash away with speed for there were too many trees around, and it was dark. Arriving at a very tall tree, they stopped there. Jay G, with his back against the tree, faced Dellen. The gun was still there pointing at him. Moving quickly, Jay G rushed into Dellen, grabbing his arm, flinging him heavily backwards. The gun went off. Jay G overpowered him, got the gun away, and dealt him some serious blows. It wasn't long before the policemen were there with torches and dogs, and took a hold on Dellen. One of the police detectives who had come along told Jay G, "Your operating ways are strange, but the results are good."

The border was just a couple kilometers away. The cars and vans of the police people turned left, and headed on the main road towards the big roundabout. A raid took place from information that Dellen had given to the police. A few men were taken in.

*

Jay G met up with the man who had given him some information when he was outside the bar that was located down in the cellar. The man had some vital news. He told Jay G where one of the top leaders was living. What Jay G had to do was check it out, find the area, and how things are situated. Jay G doesn't want the police to come in at the beginning, but he had no choice seeing that the two policemen were always with him. It was hard to get rid of them.

*

Having had a rest at home with wife and son, Jay G left to go and see what he could make of the information he had been given. He knew that the informer always told him the truth. The house Jay G came to was in its own grounds, fenced around with railings painted green. At the front were two high brick walls holding a double gate between them. There was a button along with an intercom. The two policemen weren't happy about what Jay G was doing, for the house belonged to one of their police chiefs. Or maybe Jay G had an appointment with him. They still found the way Jay G handled things very strange. Still in their car, they watched as he pressed the button at the gate. A voice came over the intercom, "Who are you?"

"Private detective Jay G." Then in a few minutes someone came from the house, looked at Jay G's ID, and let him in.

Jay G met the Chief of Police just by the door, and was taken into the front office. The chief of police offered him a chair and said, "So you're the private detective who came over from England to help with the case of the British man? I heard a lot about you."

Jay G smiled as he sat in a chair. "Good or bad?"

"You're very good in your work, I've heard."

"That's why I took on the work, to be good in it." Jay G told him.

"Why are you here?" The chief came straight to the point. "Do you want more help?"

"I don't think so, it's going well, especially with the two policemen I was given. There's no need for anymore. They'll see to it anyway!"

"So why're you here?"

"You're involved with what I'm investigating."

"Involved with what?" the chief asked. "I'm a respectful man here in my job. Everyone knows that."

Jay G shifted in his chair. "Not everyone knows your dark side."

"Come on, you can't prove a thing against me."

"Can't I?"

"I don't think you can!" the chief said.

"I have good solid information about you. You're deep in this, and I'm afraid you'll have to own up, and don't let it get worse," Jay G said.

"As a detective, you're good at making up stories. I am innocent. I have nothing to worry about."

The two policemen who were out in their car, came into the house, handcuffed Jay G, and took him away.

*

Detective Loemann came to see Jay G.

"You're digging at the wrong place, Jay G. You've brought in some good results, but *do not step over the line*. You're free to go, remember what I said. This country is not the same as where you came from. We'll back you up, when we find that your investigations have proven to be good. I think you have stepped over the line."

"You don't believe what I'm doing is good, or is it because this has to do with a police chief?"

"We know this police chief, Jay G, he's a good one." Detective Loemann said.

"That's what they say all the time, but I'm going to show you how wrong you are."

"I'd like to see that, but I think you're wrong."

Jay G was free to leave without any charges against him. He left Loemann having a worried look upon his face.

6

Jay G Takes a Big Risk

JAY G WAS now planning to not letting the two policemen know where he was. He wanted to work this out on his own which was a big risk. Two days later, he was at the house of the chief. He learned from one of the servants, that the chief was out, had gone to an important meeting. The servant gave Jay G the address where he would find the chief. Making sure he wasn't followed, Jay G made his way to the address only to learn that the chief wasn't there. Going back to the chief's house, Jay G stayed out of sight, keeping a watch on the entrance. For a long time Jay G stood there under cover, waiting for the arrival of the chief. A few minutes later, the chief's car came up to the gate, and immediately, Jay G was there at the other door of the car, he quickly opened it, and shifted himself in the seat next to the chief. Jay G was really taking a big risk not knowing what connections the car had in an emergency.

"What's this, Jay G?" the chief asked. "Have you gone crazy?"

"You know full well that you're deep in trouble, and I've got the information to prove it. Turn the car around, and follow my instructions. It would be foolish to try to get help. Just do as I say." Jay G was in command now.

The chief turned the car round and followed the directions he was given. They came off the tarmac road just at the end of the built up area, took a dirt track which came at a dead end above a quarry.

"What now?" the chief said to Jay G.

"You know well, that you're the one who gave the order to get rid of George, the British man. This you cannot deny."

"Where is your proof? You've been accusing me often, but show me *your proof!*"

Jay G noticed that when the chief stopped the car, he didn't apply the handbrakes, and the car was left in neutral. Below in the quarry were all the cranes and trucks and huts with not a soul to be seen. They were pretty high up. The chief got out of the car, and gave it a push with Jay G still inside. But Jay G had his door already unlocked for he had sensed something strange was about to take place. Jay G turned, kicking the car door hard with his right foot, at the same time slamming the brake handle on, and then flinging his whole body out the car. This was dangerous because they were very close to the edge. The car came to a halt with most of the weight at the back, and the two front wheels hanging over into the quarry below. The chief had already scrambled away, and was halfway up the track. He had his mobile on him, and immediately got into contact with his people. Jay G landed on a jagged rock which did him pain. There was no bleeding, but it was sore. Leaving the car, and making his way up the track, he saw the police cars and vans, and knew that he was in deep trouble.

*

Detective Loemann wasn't pleased meeting with Jay G again, and hearing that he had kidnapped the chief. Jay G denied that he had kidnapped the chief, but admitted that he had caused him to drive to a secluded place.

Loemann said to Jay G, "We don't kidnap people here in the Netherlands. They are driven away, and it is our task to find them."

"So what are you going to do now?" Jay G asked.

"Suspended for a week. Give you time to think carefully about the chief. You might have made a big mistake. Think carefully over that!"

Jay G realized when he got back to his apartment, and was relaxing with his wife and son, that he had not much time left in the Netherlands. He had to wrap this case up before the time finished, or he would have to stay longer.

Jay G had never been in this situation, getting suspended for a week. He knew he was right about the chief, but now he was dealing with the wrong people. They were all sticking with the chief. What can Jay G do now? That was the question, and he now know that he had to take a big risk in order to prove his case against the chief.

*

The bar that wasn't far from Jay G was just down the road, around the corner. Jay G had been there before, and the barman knew him. As he entered, with the bar on his right, the barman said, "Ah! It's you again. How's your investigation coming on?"

"Still working hard. You know, it's not easy for a detective. Give me a soft drink like the one I had before."

Jay G took the drink, went and sat down facing the door.

Twenty minutes later, and Marlene came through the door. She spotted Jay G, and went over to him.

"Hi!" she said. "How's it going?"

"Not bad," he told her. "Your information worked out well."

Marlene ordered a drink and sat with her back to the door, facing Jay G. "There is something I had not told you. I kept it to myself."

"What is that?" Jay G asked.

"I'm the mistress of the chief of police!"

She saw the look on Jay G's face.

"I've just had conflict with him, and now I've been suspended."

"You have to be careful," Marlene told Jay G. "Even though you're a detective, you can still find yourself in deep trouble. It's not an easy thing to chase people who are dealing in the stuff."

"Are you telling me that the chief is such a person?" Jay G asked.

"It could be very dangerous for me, if I answer you ..." She took a drink. "... And you won't be able to help me."

"How do you know that?"

"I just know. Trust me!"

"Are you telling me that the chief is in this dealing business? Someone has already given me some information."

"He is one of the top leaders, but he doesn't know who the top man is."

"Whatever it cost, I have to take the risk," Jay G told Marlene. "Are you sure that this chief is your lover?"

"Would I make up a story like that?"

"I suppose not. When are you going to see him again?" Jay G asked her.

"This coming Friday at my home."

"You know," Jay G said, "this is a dangerous business, but I have my work to do."

7

Confusion at Arnhem

ON FRIDAY NIGHT, Jay G was walking down towards Marlene's place. He was suspended, but not on house arrest, so he ventured out. From what Marlene had told him, he knew that the chief would be there at her place around 20:30 pm sharp. Jay G checked himself, and knew that there was something wrong. Marlene had told him that the chief would be at her place. Jay G was now wondering if Marlene had made a mistake with her information. He got to her place, pressed the button, waited, and she didn't come to the door. There were lights inside, one could see through the window curtain. He waited some more minutes, and knocked on the door itself. Still, there was no answer. Jay G had to be very careful by not leaving any fingerprints behind. He took out his gloves and put them on. Jay G eased his way in cautiously, ready for any trouble.

A little way in the corridor, he came to the living room door; it was a bit open. Jay G wasn't taking any chances. He took hold of the handle of the door, and drove it back with great force. There was a screaming noise as the inside handle rammed its way into the belly of the man behind the door. He sank down to the floor, and Jay G quickly went to him wanting to know who he was, and why he was here.

Getting the man back up, Jay G turned and saw the body of Marlene stretched out across the sofa. He quickly shuffled the man across, and saw that her neck had been broken. Jay G put his hand in his pocket, felt the mobile and pushed a button. In no time, the police were there, the ambulance as well. Loemann and a couple of detectives were there. They arrested the man, and took a statement from Jay G.

Loemann warned Jay G to stay away until his suspended time has come to an end.

"We could have arrested you for murder."

"You got to be joking," Jay G said. "As a detective, suspended or not, I was doing what was required of me."

*

The train to Arnhem was on Platform 1, and would leave in five minutes time. Jay G stepped on board, and found himself a seat. This train was headed for Amsterdam, but would stop at Arnhem. The man Loemann and the police had arrested, gave them some information. Some of it leaked out, and now Jay G was picking up on it. The information stated that there was a posh restaurant where some deals had been made. Loemann had told Jay G about it, but hadn't given him all the information he received.

Jay G concentrated deeply on the directions. He knew where he had to be. Stepping off the train in Arnhem, he found his way to the area where this posh place was.

He went in and found that tables were reserved. At one table, he saw the name *Franz Rjk* and knew immediately who it was. Jay G had no reserved table, but was allowed to stay. He ordered himself a lunch.

Just before midday, the table was occupied, but he didn't see the man who he thought was Franz Rijk there. This was now confusing; he had to find out what was going on. There were four people at the table when Jay G approached it.

"Excuse me," he said. "I'm looking for Mr Franz Rijk." A young middle-aged man looked up and said, "I'm he." Jay G was astounded. He had the wrong man.

"Sorry," he told them, "my mistake."

Jay G walked away back to where he was sitting. Jay G had seen back at the chief's house, in the office, a name written: it was Franz Rijk. In Arnhem, the description didn't fit. It had to be a thick, well-built man wearing glasses. Jay G asked the waiter if he knew Franz Rijk, gave him a description, and the waiter knew immediately who Jay G was talking about.

"That one," the waiter told Jay G, "won't be in until later today."

Jay G hung around. Out in the car park, a black Mercedes pulled in. Jay G was there right away as the man stepped out. This man fit the description well of Franz Rijk, but he wasn't the chief.

Could Jay G have got it all wrong, in that he saw the name on the chief's desk back in Nijmegen, and immediately thought that that was the chief's name? The man turned to Jay G, and Jay G asked, "Are you Franz Rijk?"

The man said, "Yes, I am. There are quite a few of us with that name!"

"That I have already experienced. Sorry to have bothered you."

"Not at all," and the man went down to the hotel.

Jay G went back to the hotel, and was in luck because there was a man there who knew that the chief from Nijmegen would be here in Arnhem. That sort of news wasn't for everyone, but how he got hold of it, was a mystery. He told Jay G of the building the chief would be in, and that it was a private meeting.

Jay G got to the building, and staked himself out. Little did he know that he had been seen, and plans were being made to find out who he was. As soon as the chief heard that it was a tall well-built man wearing a long overcoat, he knew it was Jay G.

Jay G had already moved from where he was, and was now

in a position , where he could hardly be seen. The chief had sent two men out to find Jay G, and to deal with him in anyway they could...

Jay G was lurking behind a small wooden hut when one of the men came by. Out stepped Jay G giving the man some quick punches with his right to the face, and quick ones with the left to the guts. The man sank down as the next man came to meet Jay G. He tried to get Jay G down on the ground, failed to do so, and got the taste of Jay G's right hand which was powerful. He moved away from Jay G quickly, not wanting anymore. Jay G turned and went quickly to the door of the building to try to get at the chief.

The chief could have called for help, but he didn't do so. He waited in the room, already planned what he was going to do. There were a few steps Jay G had to go up. Easing his way up carefully, he came to the door of the room. It was locked. Jay G shouted out, "Why make it harder on yourself chief? There's lots of evidence to prove that you had something to do with George. You cannot deny it anymore."

"You're done for Jay G," a voice came from the other side of the door. "Do you expect to bring such a charge against me?"

Then a gun went off, and Jay G was out the building as quick as he could. He took cover, getting out of the area quickly.

The chief had shot himself.

*

Jay G was on the train heading back to Nijmegen. He knew the news of what had happened to the chief would be all over the place. That is part of life. It wasn't long before he was off the train and going to his apartment.

At home, he learned he had permission to stay longer on the case. Jay G was hoping to get some important information from the chief, but now he had to look elsewhere. The information he wanted, was hard to get. One more day of suspension, and he'll be back in full swing.

Jay G visited some of the bars. He entered the one on the corner of Hertogstraat. It was fairly packed, but he didn't stay long. It didn't take him long to get to the bar down in the cellar. Jay G had been to a briefing, and he was given again, the two policemen as backup.

Nothing much was doing down in the cellar bar, and he left.

He walked through the archway of the old church, keeping to the left side. He came to some steps leading down to a main street. On the opposite side was a side street that would take you through the back of some buildings and bring you out to the real main street going through the town. As Jay G stepped over and entered that street, he was confronted by two men. They were on the right of him, and Jay G knew what was about to take place. He moved away swiftly from them, they followed behind. Through the small archway, out to the main road, they came to a halt when they saw the police car parked over on the other side. Jay G went up to it, told them that he was okay, and nothing to worry about. He then walked down to the bar, on the corner of the road, below the park. The police car was still keeping pace with him. He knew if there was any trouble, he had help. But he didn't really need them to be there, for they would be easily seen by anyone who was vigilant.

Anyway, it was good to know that they were there.

8

Jay G Finds Himself in Real Trouble

JUST ON THE opposite side of the bar was a street which was known as the *'red area'.* Because there was nothing much doing in the bar, Jay G went over and walked along the street. There were a few women sitting in the windows beckoning him to come in. At the end of the street, there was a man and woman acting as if they were out of their minds. They saw Jay G, as he was about to turn left and take the small side road.

"You want some stuff, man?" the man asked Jay G. Jay G said, "How much? How much?" He went up to the man and woman, then quickly he realized he was in a trap for the woman had already taken out her hand gun, and stuck it in the side of him. With his left hand in his pocket, he pushed the button on the mobile.

The man and woman led him down the dark street, and to a house. The police car was just around the corner from the bar, and hadn't seen what had happened, but knew where to go. At the house, the man and woman went up a few steps, and into the untidy room; then to a door leading below into a cellar. In this cellar there was a good deal of old furniture, lots of boxes stacked up.

They tied him to an iron ring that was attached to the wall. Jay G mobile was a special one, it always gives the exact location where he was. They hadn't searched him or anything like that. Had they done so, he would have been minus a mobile. He knew there and then that they weren't in the big game, and he had to make sure that the woman behaved herself with that hand gun. He will try not to upset her. Hurriedly, the two left, the man and the woman, and Jay G was on his own in the cellar.

The two policemen came to the house, they found the door locked. Jay G down in the cellar couldn't shout for help because they had taped his mouth. Feeling the wall with his fingers, he realized it wasn't a wall as a wall should be – solid – it was sort of *make believe* wall. Jay G twisting his wrist and tugging hoping that something would happen. Then he gave a tug, that hurt, but he kept on wriggling and tugging. Suddenly, it gave way, leaving a gaping hole there. The iron ring which was rather thin, was still attached to his hands which were tied behind his back.

*

The police car followed the man and woman in their car. They turned left as they came to the end of the road, then sped along and left again until they game to a T-junction. It was there that they were held up. On the left was a small car park, they were taken into it, and placed under arrest. They had to go back to the house, and unlock it. And there was Jay G ... still with his hands tied behind his back.

*

Two days later, Jay G was walking down the many steps at the side of the main park that was not so far away from the main bridge. The police car was at the top. They could have gone around and be at the bottom on the road of the Waal. Before Jay G got to the bottom, he was surrounded by six men, and taken to a fair-sized van at the bottom. The van sped away. Inside the van, they took everything that he had on him.

The mobile, they flung over into the water...

After ten minutes they came to a house with flowers in pots on either side of the gate fence. He was taken inside the house, and there, he came face to face with a man the same size as himself. The room was large with a desk at the far end near to a window.

"So *you're* the Jay G I've been hearing about for so long?"

"Who are you? And why am I brought here?"

"Ah! You haven't heard of me! Well, I'm in charge of Nijmegen and its surrounding area. I'm one of the bosses you see, that make sure that the clients get what they want."

"You mean illegal stuff. Doesn't the police know about you?"

"You're not up to date, are you, Jay G? You don't know how this business runs."

"I'm interested in getting those responsible for George's death behind bars," Jay G said.

The man known as Wilfred Kriss said to Jay G, "And how are you going to do that? All on your own?"

"I see that you're a funny man as well. As a detective, I'm here to do a job, and I'm going to see it through," Jay G told him.

Kriss called a couple of his men. "Show this joker out the door," he said to them. Then he said to Jay G, "I don't want *EVER* to see your face again."

"In my work, it's quite possible that you'll see me again," Jay G said, and was shown out the door.

At the police office, at a briefing, Jay G told them about Wilfred Kriss. They knew about him, and had been keeping an eye on him. Jay G took a walk across the bridge, it was a nice day. He remembered what Wilfred Kriss said when he, Jay G, had mention George's name. To Jay G, it seemed as if Wilfred Kriss knew about George, and was admitting to be part of it.

But Jay G had to be absolutely sure. He had to get himself a new mobile. The two policemen told him that they had driven around to come down to the Waal, and they came to the area where the mobile had been flung into the water. They had no other lead where Jay G was.

*

It was a real quiet day for Jay G, nothing much doing, until he was on his way home when he accidentally bumped into the informer who had given him information outside the cellar bar, next to the archway of the church. He asked Jay G how things were going on, and Jay G told him things were going good so far.

"What have you got for me this time?" Jay G asked him. He told Jay G that he has information of a dealer, he comes down from Amsterdam, and does business once a month. Jay G took the information and thanked the man.

*

One of the Dutch detectives was getting married in a couple of days time, and Jay G knew he had to be there.

*

The wedding took place in the town hall in the heart of the town. Many people were gathered there, mostly from the police and detective departments. Jay G took his wife and son along with him. After the wedding, with the information he got from the informer, Jay G found himself at the bus station waiting for the right bus to come in. He had a wait of ten minutes, and eventually, the bus he wanted, came in. The police car was nearby, he smiled to himself, knowing that help was always close by. The informer had warned Jay G that the man he was now going to see was very dangerous.

Jay G stepped off the bus after a 15-minute ride. He went

and told the two policemen to stay clear, out of sight, and to be on the alert. Jay G walked away went down a street, turned to his right, went through a street with houses on either side, then down a small track which brought him out to another road. There on the left of him was the house he wanted. At the left side of the house was a short lane leading to a small sportsfield. The front garden was as if it was hit by a bomb. He managed to find his way up to the front door, and was amazed to find that it had a push button. With his right hand finger, he pushed and waited. The door opened, and a woman showed herself.

"My husband is not in," she said. "Who are you?"

"I'm from the detective department, and I'd like to have a few words with your husband."

"He'll be back in a few minutes," she said.

As Jay G took out his badge and photo of George, the husband of the woman came along on a bike with plastic bags filled with groceries hanging from it. The wife said to her husband, "There's somebody here to see you."

He looked at Jay G. "Won't be a minute," he said, and took the plastic bags with the groceries inside. A few minutes later he was there talking to Jay G. Jay G said to him, "I'm a private detective and I'm working on the case of the British man George who was found dead down by the main bridge."

"I read about that! It was a terrible thing. How can I help you?" the man asked Jay G, leaning back on the door.

"I was thinking," Jay G told him, "you could help out should you ever hear anything that I won't be able to know."

"You mean like an informer?" He looked at Jay G more seriously and said, "No thanks, I'm not one of those."

Jay G's informer had told him that this man was dangerous. Jay G was now wondering had the informer got it all wrong. The man who was now standing next to Jay G seemed okay, and not the criminal type.

Jay G left the area, went back on the bus, accepting that this trip was a failure, nothing had turned up. Jay G took the rest of the day relaxing. He remembered what the informer had told him: *a man came from Amsterdam once a month*. Jay G rushed back to the address.

When the door was opened, the woman was there. She said to Jay G, "Oh! It's you again!" Then she turned and shouted to her husband, who came to the door. He saw Jay G standing there. "What do you want this time?"

Jay G said, "I know that you are expecting someone, and he's from Amsterdam. You lied to me."

" I don't know what you're talking about."

"I've got lots of time, I could stay around and wait." Jay G told him.

"Please yourself," he said, and closed the door.

Should the informer be right, Jay G knew that he was onto something, and was willing to hang around to see what would turn up. Jay G notified the two policemen, and they got messages back to their station. Not long after, a car turned up at the house Jay had visited. The driver had seen the police car as it turned to its left, and the driver sped away only to be confronted by a police blockage, a few meters away. The car was searched and found to have had quite a lot of stuff. The driver of the car was arrested. Jay G went to the two policemen, and thanked them for their good work. The house the man came to was searched, but nothing illegal was found.

9

The Clean-up

LOEMANN AND JAY G along with police backup went to
a certain area after they had gathered enough information.
Loemann was a good Dutch detective. He had been in the job
for sometime, and knew the ins and outs, and who was who.
Dealing with criminals, especially the dealers, he knew who
were professional, and who were not. He took to Jay G quickly,
but still didn't like the way he operated. It was quite different
from the Dutch way. As detectives, they got on well together.
The man who was arrested from Amsterdam gave away much
information after they told him that his penalty would not be
too long. Loemann knew what he had to do now. In a briefing,
he told Jay G what they were about to do.

Jay G now had all the details of the next operation. He
decided to pay a visit to the woman who lived down on the
boat by the main bridge. It was a beautiful day with the sun
beating down. She spotted him as he came close. Chairs were
already in the area on top the boat. "Never thought I'd see you
again," she said, and welcomed him up on the boat. "This time,"
she let him know, "I welcome you. You don't have to go nosing
around."

"That's what detectives do," he told her. He got onto the boat
and grabbed a chair making sure he didn't knock over the plant
pots that were nearby. Jay G didn't want anything to drink, he
only wanted to chat.

"There's something that you didn't tell me.' he told her.

"What's that?" she asked as she sat in the chair opposite. "Is it important?"

"Every piece of information is important to a detective. I found out that you and George had taken a trip on one of those passenger boats on the Waal."

"How did you know that? Yes, it is true. It was only for a few hours."

"Why didn't you tell me about it when I first talked with you?"

"I didn't think of it at the time."

Jay G said, "You did talk to me about going to a circus. In a few days time, the circus will be here again, it should bring back some memories."

"I don't think so," she said, "that's long behind me."

"I will go when it comes," Jay G said, "... and look around."

"Are you going to go and enjoy yourself like the children do?"

"I'm just interested in talking with a few people, that's all." Jay G said.

"So the case is coming on well?"

"We'll have it wrapped up sooner or later. Just a few more hurdles to cross."

"You sure you don't want something to drink?"

"I'm okay, thank you. This Karl, your boyfriend, where is he now?"

"He's on a job just across the border. He'll be back around 6 pm."

"You trust him very much, do you?"

"Yes, I do. What are you leading to?"

Jay G paused for a moment, then he said, "It is quite possible that Karl could have had something to do with George."

"That's not possible!"

"Why not?"

"Karl is a very nice man, and I trust him," she told Jay G

Jay G got up from the chair. "Thanks for the time. I'll see you around." He walked down the few steps, and came to the bottom onto the road. He walked along the harbour looking at some small passenger boats that were there. Their names were painted on the sides.

*

The day came for the big clean up. Jay G was ready and reported to the station. There were the vehicles there already waiting. The special force who always carry fire-arms were ready. Jay G knew about fire-arms. In his training, he had been shown all the different types. So he was up-to-date in that area.

Loemann had been on many of these operations, and knew what to expect. They are always dangerous, and people do get hurt. Jay G too, had been with such operations when he was back in Nottingham, they weren't new to him; he knew how to go about them.

It was an early morning raid, and Loemann had his men in their positions and waiting. Hans van de Bulin was one of these criminals who had contacts everywhere. He came down from Rotterdam, and made a name for himself dealing out stuff. The two policemen who were always there as backup for Jay G were also on this raid.

At Han's house, the party had started at 8 pm. There were many cars parked out in the yard. Well-to-do people were at this party. They were paying a good price for what Hans had to offer. But little did they know that the whole area was watched, and that the officers were ready to move in. Loemann with Jay G and a few officers went round the back. There they found a small door leading down into the bottom floor. It was lucky for them that there were no dangerous dogs around. The officers themselves had sniffer dogs.

Men and women inside were enjoying themselves, when someone accidentally peeped out the window, and saw people moving about. He alerted Hans, and straight away there was panic, he knew what was about to take place ...

Around the left hand side was another door leading upwards, and people came hurriedly out that door. A well-built man, not as tall as Jay G came out that door with a brown case in his right hand and headed for the small wire fence. On the other side was a small dug-out canal, followed by three more all in a row.

Jay G left Loemann, and moved quickly in order to apprehend the man. The man with the case got over the fence before Jay G could reach him The man strode through the canal which was not very deep, but wide and long. Jay G came out of that canal absolutely soaking wet. Behind him an officer with a sniffer dog was following. Trying hard to get over all the canals, the man himself was also wet; he got to a small farm house, and headed for the tractor. These were the type that had no keys – only a push button. He clambered awkwardly up onto the tractor, got into the seat, and hastily, he pushed the start button. As he did so, Jay G was there, holding on to the hand rail, with his right foot already on the low step. The engine of the tractor turned over, and started moving away.

Kicking out with his left foot, the man tried to get Jay G off the tractor, but Jay G had now a good hold. With his left hand, Jay G grabbed the other rail, and had now a good steady position. The tractor was now running fast across the field, and the lights came on in the farm house. It wasn't really dark, one could still see clearly. Letting go of the rail with his left hand, Jay G tried to get a grip on the arm of the man. Sometimes he would get a hold, but not strong enough to hold on. Then Jay G got a good hold on the man's arm, and he did not let go. He was tugging away like mad, but the man was strong and resisted being pulled out the tractor.

Leaving the tractor out of control, the man took his case and slammed it over the back of Jay G. He did this repeatedly. Jay G still holding on to the man's left arm, with all his strength, he gave a great tug, and got the man from behind the wheel, and onto the grass. The man wasn't easily to be overpowered, and Jay G struggled for sometime trying hard to get the upper-hand. Finally, after a few punches from Jay G, there was no more fight in the man. At the same time, the officer came by with the sniffer dog that went over to the brown case. It was found to have quite a lot of stuff inside along with letters and bills. He was handcuffed and taken away.

The farmer, in amazement, was pleased to have his tractor back without any damage to it. Loemann was pleased with the way the raid had gone. The officers who were with him had captured some people there, and had them locked in special vans ready to be taken away. Loemann met up with Jay G, and tapped him on the shoulder pleased with what he had done.

Going through the brown case, they found George's name there on a list with five others, but the man wouldn't tell them anything more. He kept still. Quite a number of people got charged for trafficking illegal stuff. An address was given and Jay G and the two policemen were sent to check it out. Back up would not be far.

The two policemen stayed out of sight, but close enough in case Jay G needed help. It was a dark dirty lane that Jay G had to walk down before he got to the address he wanted. There were about six houses; three opposite each other. He went to the right one, showed his credentials, and began talking to the occupant. Nothing intereting came out of the talk with the occupant, and Jay G didn't waste much time there.

Two days later, the circus came into town, as they always do. They started setting up their stands and equipment. Jay G waited until it was finally opened, and people began to stream in. Jay G came to the stand where the big wheel was situated, went to the small box where the attendant was. The picture of George was shown to him, and was asked if he remembered seeing him around. He remembered the face, and told Jay G about the girl who was with him. She fitted the description well of the girl down on the boathouse. There was nothing more the attendant at the big wheel could tell Jay G. Jay G went around looking at all the set-ups. He came up the area where the market usually stands on a Monday, just next to the main museum. The Belvedere hotel was just a few yards further up.

10

More Trouble for Jay G

AFTER THE CIRCUS went away, on a Monday Jay G went round the market. The two policemen in their car were keeping a close watch on what was happening, and on the movements of Jay G. There were many people doing their market shopping, and at the fish stand, there were quite a number of people buying fresh fish, and also fried ones. Jay G walked past the main museum, and as he did so, he knew that the two men who were standing at the far side of the fish stand, were now not so far behind him. Coming to the path leading to the Belvedere hotel; it split to the left and round to where the old German gun stood pointing out over the bridge. Jay G took the left path, followed it around, came and stood behind the canon of the gun, and began to look out at the beautiful site. His eyes came upon the place where they had found George. For a few seconds he tried to picture the scene around George, but nothing came through. The two men who were at the fish stand, came under the old gun, and pretended that they were looking at the scenery. One of the policemen had already left the backup car and was on his way up.

Jay G waited until the policeman came into view. He knew exactly what he was going to do, and wasted no time. He went to the tallest of the two men, swiftly tackling him, getting him over to the next level below where there was grass, both sliding down to the road. The big flower clock was not far away from them, while they both struggled and rolled, each trying to get control. Jay G was too good at this, and did not give the man a chance. The policeman at the top also had a difficult time with the other man, but got over that and arrested the man. A van was already on the way.

People over in the market place could see Jay G and the man now down at the side of the road. This road comes from the Waal next to the main bridge, up beside the market. The man was strong, he held Jay G fast, trying to break him down, but Jay G wasn't going to let that happen. Jay G was fast and gave the man a right elbow to the chin, this was something that had to be done properly, for he could have hurt his own self. Jay G then went with the finishing punches that laid the man out on the ground.

Ambulance and police vans were soon there.

At the station, Jay G was allowed to talk to the man who had the brown case, to see what he could get out of him. The man told Jay G that he had been given the task to get rid of certain people, and he would contact those who would carry it out. He would not say anymore. Jay G got the feeling that the man knew more than what he was telling him. It was like that with some of these criminals, always holding back information, hoping that it would save them. They were clever, themselves playing detectives as well. But there was one detective that could not be walked over.

Loemann cleaned up a few areas with raids, brought in about 50 people. Jay G was now thinking about the man with the brown case. Who was he giving orders to so that they could get rid of those on the list that was found in the case? Only the first names were written down, and it was hard for the police to act to protect those people. Maybe the 'George' they saw on the list had nothing whatsoever to do with George, the British man. Who knows? Jay G know now that he has to take care, for his enemies are out to get him. He can't afford to make any mistakes. In his job, it was dangerous, he was committed to it; had no regrets, and will move forward cautiously.

*

Jay G had a couple of days off so he had time to be with his wife and son. They had been well looked after by the security team. In that area, Jay G had no complaints. Jay G took a walk down to the 'cafe' that was situated on the corner from where he was staying. He had no plans of going into the place, so he passed it by, and went through the rail bridge tunnel. Walking for another 500 meters, he turns around, and began to walk back. The street lights were already on, and there were patches of dark here and there.

Coming back through the tunnel, on his right, was a small road leading to a dead end. A man stepped out in front of him, while another was just behind him. Jay G always knew when something was wrong, and immediately, he knew what he had to do.

The man in front of him was a big man; his head was massive, his neck, large, and bulging out, he was not tall though. He deliberately bumped into Jay G, while the man who was behind him, came into him from the rear. In a situation like this Jay G couldn't afford to take any chances. The two policemen were not around at this time to back him up; he was on his own. But there were many instances where Jay G was on his own, and he came out unscathed. The man behind Jay G reached up to his shoulder. He reached out and held on fast to Jay G's right hand that he had in his pocket. The man at the front grabbed Jay G's coat and was tugging as hard as he could. Jay G moved swiftly tgo the right, and then buckled himself like into a ball, and started pushing the fat man furiously forward, and into a barricaded door, that used to be a barbers shop. Still holding on, the man who was at the back tried to get his left hand around Jay G's neck, and found that he couldn't do so, he tried holding him fast around the waist.

Someone entering the 'cafe' had seen what had taken place by the archway of the rail bridge. Jay G with his left hand brought it repeatedly into the man's head like a hammer. Still the man held on, while the fat man was slumped at the barricaded door. Two policemen patrolling on bicycles came along at the same time some people came from the 'cafe.' It was all over for the two chaps who attacked Jay G.

Jay G had a soft drink, then he walked on home.

The two policemen who were always around in their patrol car to back up Jay G, were off duty, and were in the canteen. Jay G walked in and greeted them. He sat down and had a coffee. He knew that the two policemen saw clearly how he operated, and it was far from the way detectives worked in their place, but they knew he brought in good results, and had no complaints.

Jay G went around the Cozy Bar, had a soft drink. While doing so, this man came up to him and said, "So you are the detective who is working on the British case?"

"Yes, I am. And who are you?"

"I'm normally a regular here, but at the moment, I am working in Germany. Been doing so for a few months now."

"Where in Germany?"

"A place called Kleve."

"Do you know anything about the British man?" Jay G asked.

"Well, of course! He used to come here often. I spoke with him many times."

"That's interesting. What did you talk about?"

"He had this girl he used to go out with, but they broke up, and for a few weeks, he was a bit down."

"Do you know the girl's name or where she live?"

I think her name was Ingrid if I remembered rightly, and she was living with her uncle whose name was Karl."

Jay G almost spilled his drink when he heard the name. "Did you say *Karl*? Have you ever seen him?"

"I'm afraid not! But later, George, that was the Brit's name, met another girl."

"Tell me about that!"

"He came in here with her, but I don't think that it lasted long."

Jay G knew what the man was talking about. It was the girl down at the boat house whom George had met after he broke up with the first girl. Jay G said to the man, "She has a new boyfriend, and his name is Karl."

"He cannot be the same one who is uncle to George's first girl. There are quite a lot of Karls around," the man told Jay G.

11

The Pancake Boat

JAY G AGAIN shocked the two policemen who were watching from their patrol car. They weren't furious with him, for they knew he worked differently. Quickly, they got onto the police patrol boat that was a few hundred yards away, as soon as Jay G stepped onto the Pancake Boat.

The Pancake boat takes two hours to go through all the bridges along the route, and the nature reserve area. Jay G went up to the top where it was an open deck. It was a lovely day with plenty of sunshine. Here, on this boat, you are allowed to eat as many pancakes as you like. Jay G had himself a nice delicious pancake on one of those flowered dishes. As soon as he tucked in, two men came in front of him, leaning over on the table. They were about the same size as Jay G. "Enjoy your pancake," the one on his left said. But no sooner had he said so, Jay G, grabbed the plate that was on the table, and slammed it into the face of the man, at the same time, turning to the man on his right, grabbing him, tugging him over to the side where he was. The man went crashing on the floor, while Jay G moved out from between the bench and the table, and dealt more severely with the man on his left. They both tumbled to the other side of the deck, while passengers quickly moved away. Just beside Jay G and the man, was a triple-pipe-barrier as a protection all around the top deck. Here, Jay G struggled with the man, they both stood up wrestling awkwardly, and there they were, both hanging over the pipe-barrier, and suddenly, over they went and down into the water. The police patrol boat was right on hand, and picked up Jay G and the man. Jay G had known before the two men came to his table, that something was wrong. It turned out that the two men were accomplices of Hans.

*

Jay G was now putting all the pieces of information together. A picture was forming. George had been involved with something far too big for him. Jay G screwed his face up, he would have to go and see what George's first girlfriend's uncle had to say, and if his luck was in, have a word or two with the girl herself.

*

Jay G found the address, and knocked on the door with the knob that was there. The door opened, and a man appeared. Jay G guessed that the man was in his forties. After seeing his credentials, the man let him in, asked if he wanted something to drink. Jay G said, "No thanks," and sat down in the seat the man showed him. The man was very friendly, and Jay G tried not to upset him.

"I read in our papers about a detective that is coming from England to help our detectives here with the British man case."

"I am that detective," Jay G told the man. "I want to ask you a few questions."

"Go right ahead, and if I could answer them, I would gladly do so," the man replied.

"Did you meet the British man? And if you did, what were your impression of him? Was he a nice fellow?"

"I'm the girl's uncle, and she's been living with me for some time now. She's out working. Yes, she brought the British man here a long time ago. They didn't stay together very long, and I hadn't the chance to get to know him better."

"Have you any idea who might have wanted to get rid of George?"

"I'm sorry, but I'm not a detective, I leave that all to you people."

"Did you know why they broke up?" Jay G asked.

"The story I heard from her is that she had planned to meet him at the Cozy, but had come back late from a visit to Amsterdam. She didn't turn up. The next time he met her, they had a big row over it, and it fell apart between them," the man told Jay G.

"Life is funny," Jay G said. "This is something that happens all the time, especially between young lovers. Are you still working?"

"No. I'm retired, but I have a nice hobby, stamp collecting."

"Expensive!"

"Sometimes."

"Well, I should be going." Jay G got up out of his seat, gave the man a card, and told him if he remembered anything important that might help the case, he could give him a ring."

Outside the door, Jay G said to the man, "I'll come along another time and talk with the girl."

The man told Jay G that she was home on a Friday afternoon.

Climbing the small road from the lower part of the town, Jay G got to the top in time to see some policemen and an ambulance on the left of him. He went over to inquire what was happening, only to find that they were taking away the man who had always given information to Jay G. Someone had beaten him up badly.

The big criminal boss who was responsible for the distribution of the stuff throughout the Netherlands and other places was raging when he heard what Jay G had done to some of his men. "Who is this Jay G?" he asked, wanting to know more about him. "Operating without a gun? That's *ridiculous*." Jay G was in the way, and the criminal boss wanted him out, no matter what. But it wasn't that easy to get rid of him. One of the big moments would arrive when the police would have in their keeping, the man behind all this racketing. So far, they didn't know who he was. They suspected certain people of course. No one is spilling the beans. This criminal boss had caused many people to die including young ones who were addicted to the stuff. All this was done illegally. Being that sort of detective he is, Jay G has gotten very close in finding out who this criminal boss is. There's going to be a big explosion, when he gets to the heart of it. Quite a number of people would be arrested with still many more to convict. Such an operation is never easy.

12

The Trip to Düsseldorf

THE BUS WAS there by the Tunnel bridge taking on passengers in the early hours of the morning. Jay G boarded the bus, and sat at the back. His two policemen guards could not come with him, but Jay G had all the information he needed.

The Düsseldorf police were informed of his coming. The journey was only 95 kilometers away. It was nice to be out and visiting another place. Jay G thought. On his arrival back, he would go and chat with the girl who is living with her uncle, maybe something will come out of that.

Jay G was looking forward to this trip because he was going to meet someone who had lots to offer when it came to information about the stuff.

In Düsseldorf, Jay G met the man who was going to show him around, and give him information. They had lunch in a restaurant. The man gave Jay G vital information, and he learned a lot about how the stuff move around from one place to the next.

There was a man following them, and Jay G already had his eyes on him, but said nothing. Jay G told the man with him to keep walking ahead of him, and don't look back. Jay G slid into a side street, and as the man came by, Jay G grabbed his arm and tugged him in.

"Why are you following us?" Jay G asked him.

"I'm not following anyone," the man replied. "Just minding my own business."

"It doesn't look that way to me," Jay G told him.

There were many people around, and there was nothing Jay G could do, but let the man go.

The man who met Jay G at the start, and had given him information, told him some more. Apparently, there was a top man, who they knew as the boss was from Nijmegen, and working in the town's council. Jay G wanted names, but the man could not provide one. He gave only the information that he knew.

At the end of the day, Jay G got enough information to set him to work when he got back.

*

Back in Nijmegen on the Friday afternoon, Jay G went to have a chat with the girl who lives with her uncle. He found her at home, and listened to her story of meeting George. Asked how she felt when she heard what they had done to George, she said that it shocked her. It was horrible. Jay G was satisfied after questioning the girl and her uncle, that they had nothing whatsoever to do with the murder of George.

Up at the Cozy Jay G sat down outside, and had a soft drink. A young girl came by started chatting with him. "Are you the detective from Nottingham?" she asked.

"That's me," Jay G answered. "Have you got a case that I can work upon?"

"Maybe you can see what my boyfriend is doing now." She laughed. Are you on this British case?"

"Yes, do you know anything about it?"

"Only read it in the papers."

"Are you a regular here? Did you know the British man?" Jay G asked.

"No. Not personally. I saw him come in a few times with a girl, that's all."

Jay G got up to leave. "Thanks for the chat," he said, and walked over and around the corner where the two policemen were in their car. He had a five-minute chat with them, then went down the main street where the town's council building was.

It had now hit Jay G right to the core that the man he was looking for held a top job in the town. No name had been given to him, and Jay G had now to move very cautiously. The two policemen knew nothing about the high official, but the way Jay G was acting, they suspected something in that area.

Jay G came to the building, and saw the archway on the right where the cars drove in and out. He is making his plans now what he is going to do. Tomorrow is another day, and that's where it will start. He left the building, walking slowly down the road until he got to the Plein, then turned right, and down to Kronenburg park. Jay G called it a day, and went to where he was staying.

13

Jay G Meets the Criminal Boss

THE CRIMINAL BOSS had a meeting with all his men. He wanted them to bring Jay G before him. How can one man be giving us so much trouble, he told them; and not wearing any weapon as well. They told him that Jay G was a good detective, and knew how to handle himself when in trouble. The boss told them that all detectives were good, they were trained to be good. I want this one so I can deal with him myself.

No one knew who the criminal boss was, but he was functioning as a member of the town's council. It was all kept secret. Only those who knew what he was doing, like his close associates, knew his secret. Everyone knew too, that he was very wealthy, but they knew not where it all came from. His dealing in the stuff brought in quite a lot of money, people suffered as well.

Jay G paid a visit down at the boat house. He told the girl that at first, he had suspected Karl, her boyfriend, as being involved with George. Later, he changed his mind after he found new evidence.

It has now become clear to Jay G that orders were given from higher up to get rid of George. But it was not clear who was giving those orders. Jay G had to find out.

At knocking off time Jay G watched as cars came tumbling out of the town's compound, and on their way home. The following day early Jay G was there at the town's compound, and watched as the cars came in. He was at this time interested in one particular car.

As the car parked up, Jay G was there. The two policemen in their car were parked just outside from the entrance. They couldn't see within the compound what was happening. The man stepped out of the car, and Jay G was right there in front of him.

"Can I have a quick word with you?" Jay G asked him.

"Yes, why? Who are you? I have to hurry for a meeting," he said.

Jay G questioned the man for a few minutes, but nothing important came out of it.

Coming out of the compound yard, and onto the main road, Jay G spotted the two policemen who were there and waiting in their car. He went up and had a word with them.

Walking down from the town's council building, and leading down to the Plein, a car pulled up beside jay G. The driver said to him, "My boss wants to see you badly. You can come peacefully, or we have to force you, take your pick."

There were two other men inside the car – one beside the driver – and one in the back seat. They were not the friendly type, they were as mean as hell. Ready at any time to start trouble. But they hadn't seen the two policemen in the patrol car, way back behind. Jay G said to the driver, "Tell your boss, go to hell! If he wants to meet me, let him come openly right on this Plein."

The right door opened, and the left back door opened. The police patrol car was there on the spot. They got the men who were in the car onto the side, and spoke with them. Then they let them drive away. Jay G thanked the policemen for their assistance. He climbed into the police car with the two policemen, and they went after the three men, keeping a good distance, and out of sight.

The three men sped under the Tunnel bridge, and then took the first right. Jay G was let out just before that. He walked the rest of the way. He saw the car parked up, but didn't know where they were. Jay G kept himself hidden behind a post at the furniture place, looking for signs of the men. There were a number of houses there, and it was hard to tell which one they had gone into. The police car was just around the corner by the bakery.

Jay G had no special phone or anything on him, to aid him if he was in trouble. He was taking a big risk. He knew he had the police car close at hand, but the chance was there for things to go wrong. Still standing behind the post at the furniture place, Jay G had his eyes on a house with a garage on its right side.

Just as he was about to move away, two men came up beside him from out of the furniture place. Jay G had seen them come out, but it was too late for him to do anything. They had guns and were dangerous criminals. Jay G was hoping now, if only the policemen could look down his way, but that was not possible. The road had turned a corner from the furniture place, and the policemen would not give themselves away by being seen. There were no communication between Jay G and the police car. He was desperately hoping, that one of them might venture down that path.

The two criminals got Jay G over to the house where the other one was. There weren't many people around in that street, so it was easy to do what they were doing. Into the garage they took Jay G, then into the car that was parked there. It was one of those up-to-date fast cars.

Out of the garage, the car came, the driver turning to the

right, and headed for the traffic lights about 20 meters ahead. Just around the corner was the police car. The two policemen sat in the car with their backs towards the traffic lights. Their car was facing the other way. As soon as the car from the criminals came to the lights it changed to green, and they drove through, heading for the tunnel bridge. One of the policemen happened to turn around just in time to see the car. They saw Jay G at the back between two men. Turning their car around quickly, they got in the same direction as the criminals, but they had long gone. The police car was really fast. They set their siren on. Messages were already sent to other patrol cars.

Through the tunnel bridge the criminals' car sped until it came to the first traffic lights. Then it went up and around the round-about, and took the Arhnem road. Just before the bridge, it took a right leading to Germany. The police car was still some distance behind, and they hadn't seen that the car had taken a right turn. The police car went across the bridge, but turned off as soon as they realized the the criminals car hadn't come this way. On its way back, the police car took the left turn that would also take them to Germany.

After about one kilometer, the criminal car took a left and went down that road where it came to a house with double garages. Automatically, the garage door was raised, and the car went inside, and out of sight.

Jay G was taken out the car, up some stairs, into a big room where a well-built man was sitting in a chair. He got up to meet the men and Jay G. Jay G said to the man, "You've done a foolish thing by bringing me here."

"Oh, I had to see you personally," the man said. "I am Geert Kaas, and I must be the man you really want to see."

"I only deal with criminals to bring them to justice."

Geert Kaas told his men that they could now leave him

alone, and they left him and Jay G and went away.

The room was very elegant and done out well. Geert Kass showed Jay G the chair, and Jay G took it. Jay G looked at Geert Kaas, and asked, "What are you planning to do now? You've got me in your power, or so you might think, and you can do whatever you like with me. Why is it that criminals always think that they have power? And in the end, it is taken away from them."

"It is plain to see," Geert Kaas said, "that you have no power now. Where is help going to come from for you?"

"Are you going to get rid of me like you did with George, the British man? How long can you carry on in this dirty business?" Jay G spoke back.

"The man George was a fool. He didn't realize that he was playing a dangerous game with his threats."

"How many more innocent people have you gotten rid of? You are working in the town council, and yet you're corrupt, dealing in stuff, and killing people. Does any of your colleagues know about this, or are they in it with you?"

Geert Kaas had been leaning back on his desk, when he half turned to take up something from it. Jay G saw his chance, and moving quickly, grabbing the right hand of Kaas, and taking the gun that he had on him away. Both men struggled for a while, and Jay G being the tallest of the two had the advantage, and he used it perfectly well. Kaas was strong, not giving in, he fought back. Jay G had already punched a code with his left hand into the mobile that was lying there. Kaas being pushed down upon the desk, heaved himself up a bit, and both men went flying on the floor, knocking things on the desk over. Jay G tried to hold him against the leg of the desk, but Geert Kaas got the better hand and escaped being held by Jay G. Up on their feet, still holding on to each other, Jay G pulling as hard as he could, brought Geert Kaas crashing into a book cabinet. As Jay G tried to pick Kaas up, he found himself being dragged down and held in a tight tackle. Getting out of that tackle, Jay G, half lifted Kaas, and rammed him into the side panel causing a great crashing of ornaments falling to the floor. And it must have been from this that the other criminals heard the noise.

They came rushing in, with their guns in their hands. Jay G had no choice but to let Kaas go. Getting up from the floor, Kaas gave Jay G a few punches in the guts. "I never liked detectives," he said.

Just then the front door bell rang. Kaas opened it, and detective Loemann along with policemen rushed in. Outside there were police vans and cars. Loemann went to Jay G, and asked if he was okay. Jay G gave Kaas an enormous backhander and said, "Keep away from detectives."

The criminal men were taken away. Jay G handed over the gun he had taken away from Kaas.

The case of the British man was wrapped up.

If you've enjoyed this book …

Jay G 978-1-78222-656-7

Also by John Gumbs

Jehanne 978-1-78222-571-3
The Trial and Burning of Jehanne 978-1-78222-609-3
Aitch H 978-1-78222-628-4
Heidi 978-1-78222-682-6
Sheila 978-1-78222-729-8
Just Mates 978-1-78222-751-9

www.ingramcontent.com/pod-product-compliance
Lightning Source LLC
Chambersburg PA
CBHW070808120626
46557CB00002B/767